A Fish Story

by

Jon Tuttle

SAMUEL FRENCH

FOUNDED 1830

NEW YORK HOLLYWOOD LONDON TORONTO

SAMUELFRENCH.COM

ISBN 978-0-573-65240-0   Printed in U.S.A.   #8701

IMPORTANT BILLING AND CREDIT REQUIREMENTS

A FISH STORY was first produced by the University of New Mexico Summerfest, June 6, 1985, and again by the UNM Department of Theatre Arts, October 25, 1985. It was directed both times by Wade Stevens. The casts and crews were, respectively:

GEORGE . . . . Ray Rahner/Al Jones

ZEE . . . . Katy Ryan "KT" Martin/Krista Page

ANNIE . . . . April Lawrence/Renata Gregori

FRANK . . . . Graham Scott Green/Tanner Parsons

Assistant Director . . . . Jenny Gardham

Scene Designer . . . . Roy Hoglund

Lighting Designer . . . . Jason Sturm/Kare Boyce

Stage Manager . . . . Charles Baird/Anastasia Rokicki

The author remains very grateful to Wade Stevens for his wisdom, friendship and superior comic timing; to Robert Hartung, our mentor, who is now legend; and most particularly to Graham Scott Green, who as Artistic Director at Murphy's Creek Theatre remembered, requested and directed this play in 2004, thereby inspiring this revision and re-publication. Cheers to you, Scott, and to everyone at Murphy's Creek.

The playwright is a member of the Dramatists Guild.

CHARACTERS

GEORGE, the father
ZEE, the mother
ANNIE, their teenage daughter
FRANK, about nineteen

SETTING

A well-appointed cabin in the mountains. In the front room is a couch long enough to seat three uncomfortably, a coffee table, a hope chest, a fireplace and other stuff. Exits to the kitchen on one side and bedrooms on the other. There's a small rug by the front door, which exits onto a long porch. A window looks out into the woods.

TIME

Late fall, last year.

ACT ONE

*In **darkness**: we hear muffled gunshots somewhere in the distance. Then silence. Then more gunshots.*

*At **rise**: mid-afternoon: **ANNIE**, a teenage girl, is on the couch, half-heartedly knitting a beat-up afghan. **ZEE**, her mother, is standing at the window anxiously.*

ZEE. …Idiot. …God!

ANNIE. I wouldn't stand too close to that window.

ZEE. I don't know why he thinks he needs a gun. He's going to hurt somebody, you watch. He's going to blow his own foot off. Or his leg. Or his head, that'll teach him, he's going to blow his own –

ZEE suddenly realizes what she's saying and is horrified.

ANNIE. …I know, Mama. It's okay.

ZEE. …I just…I just wish he'd come back.

ANNIE. How's this?

She means the afghan, which she holds up.

ZEE. …It's too tight, Annie. Why do you always make it so tight? It's not a blanket, it's an afghan. It has to breathe. Here.

ZEE takes the afghan and pulls out a row of stitches.

ANNIE. Mama! That took me, like, an hour!

ZEE. Watch me. It shouldn't take you an hour. Don't pull so hard. It's like you're trying to strangle it to death.

ZEE is horrified again.

…God I keep doing it.

ANNIE. Stop thinking about it.

7

ZEE. I know. …I just…wish he'd….

> **ZEE** *begins to tremble.*

ANNIE. (*gently*) …Mama.

> *Boom! The door bursts open and there's* **GEORGE***, the father. He places his shotgun beside the door and holds out a furry, bloody carcass.*

GEORGE. …Well? Well? Whattaya say now, huh?

ZEE. George, good Lord!

GEORGE. Huh? Huh? How about *this?*

ANNIE. Daddy!

ZEE. What have you done!

GEORGE. They said he couldn't do it! They said he'd never be a hunter! And here he is!

ZEE. What *is* it?

GEORGE. It's a wolf!

ZEE. It's bleeding on the rug!

GEORGE. Or a coyote. Look at his teeth!

ANNIE. It's a *dog!*

GEORGE. Or a fox.

ANNIE. It's a *dog!*

GEORGE. It's a dingo! Or a, or a –

ANNIE. It's a dog, it's a dog, it's wearing a collar! It's a dog! Put it down!

ZEE. Pick it up!

ANNIE. You shot a *dog!*

ZEE. Oh my God!

GEORGE. It was on our property!

ZEE. This isn't our property!

ANNIE. How could you shoot a dog!

GEORGE. It was comin' right at me! It was wild! Look at his –

ZEE. Get out! Just get it out! Go! Go put it somewhere!

> **ZEE** *runs* **GEORGE** *out the front, slamming the door*

behind him. She and **ANNIE** *look at each other – and* **ANNIE** *flees to the bedroom, crying.* **ZEE** *waves her fists, contorts and scowls in silent fury, picks up a pillow or something soft and batters it against the couch, and then picks up something breakable, like a vase, and holds it up as if to smash it on the floor. She stays in that position, shaking, then returns it to its place. She straightens, forces a pleasant smile and perfect composure, then returns to the couch and begins knitting, quietly humming.*

GEORGE *enters again, contritely. Pause.*

GEORGE. ...Well?

ZEE. "Well" what.

GEORGE. ...Go ahead. Let's get it over with.

ZEE. (*knitting happily away*) ...I feel...I feel I don't. ...I can think of nothing to say. To commemorate this occasion. To capture the...there are no words, really. ...Is there anything *you'd* like to add?

GEORGE. ...His name was Fritz.

ZEE. Fritz. What a happy name. And do we know to whom Fritz belonged?

GEORGE. The Keefers.

ZEE. The Keefers! They sound delightful.

GEORGE. I need a beer.

GEORGE *exits to kitchen.* **ZEE**'s *knitting speeds up.*

ZEE. You're going to have to call them. I'd want to know it if somebody whacked *my* schnauzer.

GEORGE. (*calling from off*) Hey Bucky! How 'bout a beer!

ZEE. Leave her alone.

GEORGE. (*off*) How 'bout you and me go out and dig some worms!

ZEE. She doesn't want to dig worms with you.

GEORGE. (*off*) We're gonna go out and do us some fishin' tomorrow, ain't that right, Bucky?

ZEE. It'll rain.

GEORGE. (*off*) "It'll rain." You wish it'll rain.

ZEE. It will. I can feel it.

GEORGE. (*off*) "I can feel it."

> *A distant clap of thunder.* **GEORGE** *returns with two beers.*

> …So what! Little rain never hurt anybody. Cleans out your pores. – Ain't that right, Bucky! Got a beer here for ya!

ZEE. Just stay where you are, Annie!

GEORGE. Put hair on your chest!

ZEE. Quit giving her beer, George! She's still a child!

GEORGE. You treat her like a baby.

ZEE. You treat her like a man.

GEORGE. Time I was her age, I could drink a beer through my nose. – Come on Bucko! Bottoms up! It's good and it's good *for* you!

> *He takes a swig.*

ZEE. Just ignore him, Sweety.

GEORGE. Aah! Lovely bouquet, smooth aftertaste.

ZEE. Ow!

GEORGE. Stab yourself there dear?

ZEE. Shut up.

GEORGE. Better put some beer on it.

ZEE. Would you just go *away*!

GEORGE. You go away! Old bat!

ZEE. Cave dweller!

GEORGE. Varicose veins!

ZEE. Grow up!

> **ANNIE** *storms through the room and exits out the front. Pause.*

ZEE. …Well. I hope you're happy now. Mr. Big Shot Puppy Killer.

GEORGE. I *am* happy. I've had a *great* day.

ZEE. Where did you put it?

GEORGE. By the woodpile. – Hey Snake-Eye!

This last out the door, after **ANNIE**.

ZEE. She hates those stupid names you call her.

GEORGE. Hey Cochise! Where the hell'd you go?

ZEE. And do you have to swear all the time? She hears you, you know.

GEORGE. Haul some damned wood in while you're out there, would ya?

ZEE. (*calling*) You stay away from that woodpile, Annie!

GEORGE. Would you give it a rest, please!

ZEE. It's your fault! We were sitting here knitting! We were –

GEORGE. "We were sitting here knitting! We were sitting here knitting! We were sit – "

He snaps up the afghan – and realizes:

…This is *his*.

ZEE. …It has holes in it.

GEORGE. We don't need this thing around here, Zee.

ZEE. I can fix it!

GEORGE. I can fix it too. I'll show you how we fix this.

He takes the afghan and heads out the front door, grabbing his shotgun on the way.

ZEE. Give it back! Wait! That's Robbie's! That's *Robbie's!*

Standing on the porch, **GEORGE** *throws the blanket onto the ground just beyond.*

GEORGE. His name ain't Robbie!

He pumps.

It's Bob!

Blam! He fires. At that moment, **ANNIE** *enters the porch. At the blast, she screams and falls.* **ZEE** *comes running.*

ZEE. Annie!

GEORGE. Bucky?

ZEE. George, dammit! You've really done it this time!

GEORGE. I didn't see – ! I was just – ! She was – !

General pandemonium as **ANNIE** *limps onto the porch.* **ZEE** *rushes to her.*

ZEE. Annie! My baby! Oh, God! She's covered in blood! You've *maimed* her!

ANNIE. I think I'm okay.

GEORGE. You okay, Big Guy?

ZEE. Just keep away, you moron! Go shoot some cows!

They all enter the cabin as a parade – first **ANNIE,** *then* **ZEE,** *then* **GEORGE.**

ANNIE. I think I'm okay.

ZEE. You're limping. He's crippled you and you'll have to use a walker!

ANNIE. No, I just fell and skinned my knee.

ZEE. Sit down! I'll get some bandages or something.

ANNIE. No, I just –

ZEE. Your body has been mang – I'm going to pass out.

ANNIE. Sit down, mother.

ZEE. We've got to *do* something.

ANNIE. I'll get an icepack.

ZEE. Icepack, yes. Icepack.

ANNIE exits to the kitchen. Pause. **GEORGE** *has been skulking around by the door, holding his shotgun.*

GEORGE. Zee? …I –

ZEE. (*meaning: "not one word"*) Huuuhhhppp!

ANNIE re-enters with an icepack. She will sit next to her mother and apply the icepack to her own knee, but **ZEE** *will take it and put it to her own forehead.*

GEORGE. You okay there Butch?

ZEE. Don't you dare answer to that.

GEORGE. *What!*

ZEE. *Look!*

> **FRANK** *is hanging onto* **ANNIE.**

GEORGE. Ho – ly!

> **GEORGE** *grabs his shotgun.*

FRANK. Aaaaarrrrhh!

ANNIE. Can you stand!

FRANK. My leg! It's my leg!

GEORGE. (*aiming*) Get offa my daughter, boy!

ZEE. George for God's sake no!

FRANK. (*utterly terrified*) Aaaaaaaaaah!

GEORGE. Annie, get away from there!

ANNIE. Daddy wait! He's hurt!

GEORGE. Move! Move!

> **ANNIE** *backs away from* **FRANK,** *leaving him struggling to stand.*

FRANK. Aaaaaa! Ow! Ow!

GEORGE. You! Throw that pack down! Do it! …Now turn around!

> **FRANK** *complies, petrified.*

ANNIE. Daddy!

GEORGE. Up against that wall! Over there! Now spread 'em!

FRANK. Do what?

GEORGE. Spread 'em! Spread 'em! Like this!

> **GEORGE** *demonstrates, and* **FRANK** *spreads 'em.*

ZEE. George, you're scaring him.

FRANK. I can explain!

GEORGE. *Did I ask you to talk?*

FRANK. *No sir!*

GEORGE. When I want you to talk, I'll say talk, so you know! Okay? …*Talk!*

FRANK. Okay!

GEORGE. Okay! – Zee, get over there and frisk him.

ZEE. Do what?

GEORGE. Frisk him! Check his sleeves, check his coat!

ZEE. For what?

GEORGE. Just do it! – Annie, see what he's got in that pack.

ANNIE. Would you just hold on for one –

GEORGE. *Just everybody quit arguing with me!* I can only do one thing at a time! Now do it!

    ZEE *frisks* **FRANK** *politely.*

ZEE. It's a very nice jacket.

FRANK. Thank you.

ZEE. Rayon, isn't it?

    ANNIE *is unloading the pack:*

ANNIE. One can of Spaghetti-O's, with little meatballs. One box of fuzzy things.

GEORGE. Drugs!

FRANK. Flies! They're flies. For fishing.

ANNIE. One book: *Walden, or A Life in the Woods.*

ZEE. Here's something.

    She's found a card in **FRANK**'s *coat pocket.*

GEORGE. What is it? Give it here.

FRANK. It's my fishing license.

GEORGE. This ain't your license.

FRANK. Yes it is.

GEORGE. "Francis"? The hell kind of a name is "Francis"?

ZEE. Stop swearing, George.

FRANK. It's a family name.

GEORGE. It's a girl's name.

ZEE. It's a very nice name.

FRANK. I go by Frank, sir.

GEORGE. Turn your head! …You got a *earring*.

GEORGE pumps the shotgun.

He's a *cornflake*.

FRANK. I am not!

GEORGE. Shut up! Nancy. Mary-Lou. – Zee, check his legs, empty his pockets, see what else we got here.

ZEE sighs, puts her hand in one of FRANK's pockets, and instantly recoils.

ZEE. George! Really, I can't do this!

GEORGE. Oh, move aside! I'll do it!

Keeping the gun aimed at FRANK, GEORGE quickly pats FRANK down. When he hits FRANK's injured leg, FRANK falls.

FRANK. Owwww!

ZEE. George! For God's sake!

ZEE takes over, pushing GEORGE out of the way.

GEORGE. I hardly touched him!

ANNIE. I told you, he's wounded!

ZEE. He's bleeding!

GEORGE. He's faking! – Pansy!

FRANK. I slipped on a rock – fell in the river!

ZEE. Oh you poor – he fell in the river, George!

FRANK. Carried me for – I don't know – miles! Washed up on the bank…saw this place…I'm sorry, I didn't mean to scare anyone!

GEORGE. You didn't scare anyone! Alice!

ZEE. His name is Frank.

GEORGE. Annie, here. Keep a bead on him while I go get my pants.

GEORGE hands the gun to ANNIE and exits to the bedroom. ZEE has helped FRANK to his feet.

ZEE. Are you alright?

FRANK. I don't know, ma'am. My leg. It's kinda numb.

ZEE. Annie! Bandages! In the kitchen!

> **ANNIE** *puts the gun aside and starts off to kitchen.* **FRANK** *watches her.*

FRANK. Um, hi.

ANNIE. Hi.

> *And she's gone.*

ZEE. You'll have to take your pants off.

FRANK. Ma'am?

ZEE. And your shirt. You're soaking wet, you poor thing. Go on – off with everything. I'll be right back. Here: lean on this.

> **ZEE** *hands the shotgun to* **FRANK** *and exits to the kitchen.* **FRANK** *shrugs, leans on the gun and removes his shirt, then pushes his pants to his ankles.* **GEORGE,** *now wearing pants, enters from the bedroom and stops in his tracks. Pause.* **FRANK** *holds the shotgun out to* **GEORGE***:*

FRANK. ...She made me do it.

> **GEORGE** *snatches it back.*

GEORGE. Zee! Get me some rope!

> **ZEE** *enters with a flannel shirt.*

ZEE. What are you going to do, George, hang him?

GEORGE. I'm going to tie him up!

ZEE. Oh, for Pete's sake, he hasn't done anything.

GEORGE. He trespassed on our property!

ZEE. This isn't our property! – This isn't our property. It's a time share

> **ANNIE** *enters from kitchen with bandages.*

ANNIE. Here's the bandages.

ZEE. Good. Here. Go make some coffee.

ANNIE. It's already on.

ZEE. Here, put this on.

> **ZEE** *offers* **FRANK** *the shirt.*

GEORGE. What's that? What's that you're giving him?

ZEE. Just an old shirt.

GEORGE. It's *my* shirt!

ZEE. No it isn't.

GEORGE. It isn't anybody else's!

ZEE. It's Robbie's! You gave it to him last Christmas, but it was too big.

GEORGE. So you're giving it to him?

ZEE. Are you going to wear it? – Go ahead, put it on. Does it fit alright?

FRANK. Yes ma'am.

ZEE. Good. Now this may hurt.

> *She pushes* **FRANK** *onto the couch.*

FRANK. What is it?

ZEE. Alcohol.

> *She applies it to the wound.*

FRANK. Aaaaiiiieee!

ANNIE. Mama! Be careful!

GEORGE. I'm losing my patience over here!

ZEE. Annie, go get the coffee.

> **ANNIE** *exits to kitchen.*

GEORGE. Is anybody listening to me?

ZEE. He's just a boy, George! He's hurt and he needs our help.

> **ZEE** *removes* **FRANK**'s *shoes and begins to bandage his leg.*

GEORGE. He's a grown man, and what he needs is a little backbone – you got that, Barbara?

ZEE. His name is *Frank*!

FRANK. I think I can…make it to the…highway if I –

He tries to stand; **ZEE** *pushes him back down.*

ZEE. You're not going anywhere. You'll bleed to death and catch pneumonia. Now you tell me if this is too tight.

She means the bandage. It is:

FRANK. Yaaaaah!

ANNIE *enters with coffee.*

ANNIE. Here's the coffee!

ZEE. Help him with it. Don't spill on his shirt.

ANNIE *holds the cup while* **FRANK** *sips. It burns his mouth.*

ANNIE. It's still real hot. You want some cream or sugar?

FRANK *shakes his head no.* **ZEE** *is finished with the bandage and pats it.*

ZEE. There now! How's that feel!

FRANK. *(nodding in pain and unable to speak)* Mmmm-mmmmmm!

ZEE *strips his pants off.*

GEORGE. What are you *doing?*

ZEE. Do you need anything else?

FRANK. *(frantically no)* Uhhh-uhhh-uhhhh!

ZEE. Are you hungry?

FRANK. Pants!

ZEE. I've got to soak them, and wash them, and dry them, and iron them, and patch them, and then you can have them back. Annie – take these, and get some aspirin and whatever else you can find.

GEORGE. Hold it! Hold it, just stop right there! Nobody moves until I say so. This is coming to an end right here. This boy is getting tied up. – Annie, get that yarn. I'm gonna make sure this boy doesn't perpetrate any horse hockey.

Pause. **ANNIE** *doesn't move.*

Well? ...*Move!*

ANNIE *sighs and grabs a ball of yarn.*

ZEE. He's not our prisoner, George!

GEORGE. He's not our guest, either. Annie, tie him up good and tight.

ANNIE. He's not done with his coffee.

GEORGE. I don't care! I don't care if he's done with his coffee! Just tie him up!

ANNIE *binds* **FRANK**'s *wrists and/or ankles. He watches her.*

ANNIE. ...Tell me if I'm hurting you.

FRANK. You're okay.

ANNIE. I'm sorry about this.

GEORGE. Is it tight?

FRANK. Yes sir. Real tight.

GEORGE. Not you.

ANNIE. Yes sir. Real tight.

ZEE. Not *too* tight.

GEORGE. Will you let me do this! – Okay, little girl, you go to bed now. ...Well, go on!

FRANK. ...Goodnight!

ANNIE. Goodnight.

ANNIE *exits to the bedroom. Pause.*

GEORGE. Now then. I'm going to stay right here and keep my eye on you, Francine. And I've got a friend here to help me. You know what this is?

FRANK. It's a shotgun.

GEORGE. You bet it is. It's a *big* shotgun.

ZEE. It better not be loaded.

GEORGE. Of course it's loaded, what do you think?

ZEE. Fun is fun, George, but –

GEORGE. Shouldn't you be going to bed now?

ZEE. *I'm* not going to bed.

GEORGE. You're not staying out here.

ZEE. Oh isn't this just typical.

> **FRANK** *has put his feet up on the table.*

GEORGE. What is that, what are you doing?

FRANK. Sorry!

ZEE. Oh, for goodness' sake, make yourself comfortable.

GEORGE. Get your feet off there! You made our whole family uncomfortable. Now you can be uncomfortable yourself.

ZEE. I'm not uncomfortable.

GEORGE. Will you just *go to bed!*

ZEE. I'm perfectly comfortable.

GEORGE. Out! Get out! Out! Out!

ZEE. Oh alright! But I get him in the morning!

> **GEORGE** *chases* **ZEE** *off to the bedroom. Then he turns to* **FRANK** *and scowls savagely. Here follows an uncomfortable pause.* **GEORGE** *doesn't know what to do. He tries to look like a tough guy, but then relaxes a bit. Finally:*

GEORGE. So uh. …What're you doin' up in the mountains, anyhow. Hidin' out, or something?

FRANK. No sir. Just kinda…on the road. Thought I'd take in a little fishing.

GEORGE. Oh yeah?

FRANK. Yes sir.

GEORGE. Where's your pole?

FRANK. I lost it. When I fell in the river.

GEORGE. …Oh yeah.

FRANK. Really nice one, too.

GEORGE. Mmm…. You uh…you like to fish, do you?

FRANK. Yes sir. Fly fish.

GEORGE. Fly fish. I never done that.

FRANK. Oh it's great. I could show if you want. It's really easy.

GEORGE. Don't suck up to me, boy.

FRANK. No sir. I just thought that, in exchange for your... hospitality and all, I could –

GEORGE. You just sit there and be uncomfortable and maybe I could teach *you* a thing or two. Fill you in on a few things. Bring you up to speed on a few things around here.

FRANK. Oookay.

GEORGE. Like what to do when some yahoo comes bustin' into your cabin in the middle of the night 'n tries to climb all over your daughter. I mean, it ain't anything personal, tying you up and all. You might be one helluva guy, I don't know. But it's my *job*, you understand.

FRANK. Oh, I understand, sir.

GEORGE. There are things a man *has* to do.

FRANK. That's true.

GEORGE. Hard things, you know.

FRANK. I know.

GEORGE. And women don't *understand* that sometimes. They don't understand the, the, the –

FRANK. – pressure –

GEORGE. The *pressure* of, of, what it means to be a, a, a –

FRANK. – man.

GEORGE. That's right.

He sighs, frustrated.

...I'm going to have to keep you tied up like that, you know.

FRANK. Of course.

GEORGE. And I don't know if it's right to be talkin' to you like this.

FRANK. Whatever you –

GEORGE. I don't gotta explain nothin' to you!

FRANK. No sir.

GEORGE. ...Alright. We're just gonna sit here, then.

...Coupla wooden Indians. ...Not say a word. Not another word....

GEORGE *gets up, if he was sitting, and looks out the window. Long pause. Then he turns and looks at* **FRANK,** *who is just sitting there, uncomfortable.*

...You uh...you want a beer?

End scene.

Scene 3

At rise: a few hours later. The scene change is as short as possible. As lights come up, **GEORGE** *and* **FRANK** *are sitting on the back of the couch.* **FRANK** *is unbound and wearing the afghan like a skirt. They are drunk or almost, and* **GEORGE** *is trying to convince* **FRANK** *to have another beer:*

GEORGE. What the hell, come on, come on, Francis, ya pansy, one more, one more, Francis, come on, okay, okay – (*etc.*)

FRANK. (*simultaneously*) No, no, no more, really, no, I can't, quit calling me that, no, okay, what the hell, okay, one more, okay, okay, okay – (*etc.*)

They open beers and drink.

Okay. Where was I?

GEORGE. The fishsticks –

FRANK. The Physics –

GEORGE. The Fishics –

FRANK. – of fishing.

GEORGE. Right.

FRANK. Whereby: you have axioms, maxims and postulates.

GEORGE. Axles, maximums and prostitutes.

FRANK. Prostitute Number One: Fish…cannot eat and spawn at the same time.

GEORGE. I can.

FRANK. Prostitute Number Two: Fish…are very picky about what they eat.

GEORGE. I'm not.

FRANK. Third and final Prostitute: Fish…are basically ruthless loners, cannibals, heartless little bastards. But when the river runs high, they huddle together behind rocks.

GEORGE. So beautiful.

FRANK. Therefore: the shortest distance between a fish and a frying pan…is a straight nylon line. In the correct place. With the correct bait. As determined by specific seasonal and topographical variables. And the kind of mood the fish is in.

GEORGE. So complicated.

FRANK. Man and the elements. Co-existing in harmony.

GEORGE. Show me that fly thing again.

FRANK. Again? We've done it a hundred –

GEORGE. On more, ya pansy, come on, one more, one more, come on, come on, okay, okay, okay – (*etc.*).

FRANK. (*simultaneously*) No, no, no, come on man, we already, we, no, no, okay, one more, one more, okay, one more, okay. Get the fly rod.

GEORGE. Fly rod.

From behind the couch or somewhere, **GEORGE** *retrieves the shotgun. A few feet of yarn dangle from the end of the barrel.*

FRANK. Okay. Now hold it in your right hand, line in your left. Got it? Okay. Now just tease 'em with it, nice and easy. Like throwing.

GEORGE. Okay, I got it.

GEORGE *whips the line through the air.*

FRANK. No no no, you're going too fast again, George. You don't whip 'em to death. You've got to tempt 'em with it…place it…right on top…count to three. One.

GEORGE. Onetwothree.

FRANK. Two. Three.

GEORGE. Oh. Slow.

FRANK. Place it again, watch for the silver, the flash of silver.

GEORGE. That's the fish.

FRANK. That's the fish. Soon as you see it – quick jerk! That'll set the hook before he gets a chance to spit it out.

GEORGE. One. Two. ...I see it! I see the silver!

> **FRANK** *has been hooking an empty beer can to the "fly" at the end of the line.*

FRANK. Quick jerk! Quick jerk!

GEORGE. Quick jerk!

FRANK. Bring him in! Don't let him get away!

> **GEORGE** *pulls while* **FRANK** *tugs at the can: an epic struggle.*

GEORGE. He's puttin' up a fight!

FRANK. Keep the line taut!

GEORGE. Get in here, you bastard!

FRANK. Don't give him any slack!

GEORGE. I'll get him!

FRANK. Get him, George! Get him! Bring him in! (*Etc.*)

> **FRANK** *releases the can, and* **GEORGE** *"nets" or grabs it.*

GEORGE. *I got him*! Alright! Okay! They said he couldn't do it!

FRANK. Okay! That's good…. Now: what is it.

GEORGE. It's a…rainbow trout. A brook trout. A carp. I don't know.

FRANK. How big is it?

GEORGE. (*reads the can*) 'bout…twelve ounces.

FRANK. And it's got teeth…so it must be a…

GEORGE. A dyke!

FRANK. A pike! A pike!

GEORGE. A pike! A pike! Right! Let's do it again! Come on, one more, one more, what the hell, come on!

FRANK. No, come on, really, no, no more, we've been fishing for hours, George. How many we got?

> **GEORGE** *produces a stringer loaded with empty beer cans.*

GEORGE. About twenty five.

FRANK. Ah, see. Bad news. This river is out of fish.

GEORGE. Oh no.

FRANK. Oh yes.

GEORGE. So let's throw 'em back, catch 'em again.

FRANK. Oh they won't bite again.

GEORGE. Sure they will.

FRANK. No they won't. Too smart.

GEORGE. Fish sure as hell are not smart. If fish are so smart, how come they eat their own babies?

FRANK. I didn't say they were great parents. What I said –

GEORGE. Fish are so smart, how come they eat this? Don't look like no fly to me.

FRANK. It's a mosquito. Fish love mosquitoes. They bite down on that expecting a delicacy, but what they get is a cold, hard hook through their cheek, and a taste of their own blood.

GEORGE. I didn't even know they had tongues.

FRANK. You can throw 'em back, but that taste stays in their mouth. They'll never bite another mosquito.

GEORGE. …Pfffff.

FRANK. I mean really. Would you?

GEORGE. I don't eat mosquitoes.

FRANK. But think about it. I mean, what's life? What is life?

GEORGE. That's a good question.

FRANK. It's a *damned* good question.

GEORGE. Damned good question.

FRANK. What is life?

GEORGE. It's a *great* question.

FRANK. I'm asking, George! What is it?

GEORGE. I don't know! How the hell do I know? I just found out fish had tongues!

FRANK. Alright. I'll show you what it is. Watch this. Take that pike there and throw it on the floor.

GEORGE. Mother'd kill me.

FRANK. She'll never know. Go ahead. Grab him by the gills. Now put him on the rug.

> **GEORGE** *puts the beer can onto the floor and watches it carefully.*

GEORGE. Okay.

FRANK. Now – what's he doing?

GEORGE. He's uh…floppin' around.

FRANK. Step one: Denial. "I am not dying." Look him in the eye. Go ahead, you'll see it. "I am not dying."

GEORGE. (*to the "fish"*) You're *dying*, bub.

FRANK. What's he doing now.

GEORGE. Sorta…twitchin'.

FRANK. Step two: Defiance. "I will not die. I will not die! I refuse!" And he'll lie there, with that gleam in his eye, like he's looking out at something far, far away. And at that moment George, at this very crucial moment, he begins to have something we don't.

GEORGE. Rigor mortis.

FRANK. Death Perception.

GEORGE. Huh?

FRANK. Death Perception. Total fish consciousness. The sum total of his entire fish life, all bound together in each last, desperate fish breath. The hatchery where he frolicked as a minnow, the taste of a grasshopper, the thrill of a waterfall, his first fertilization. Warm currents, cool eddies, the shadow of leaves floating by – everything! In one mystical, transcendent fish moment…. No, if you want that fish, George, you better take him now. 'Cause he won't bite again. He's got Death Perception.

> *Pause.*

GEORGE. …You're one a' them college boys, ain't ya.

FRANK. Yeah. Well, I was. I quit.

GEORGE. Good for you.

FRANK. Because what is life, George?

GEORGE. I forget.

FRANK. It's life. Life is just life. And that's all it is.

GEORGE. ...Well hell. I *knew* that.

FRANK (*referring to his book*) That's what this Thoreau guy taught me. He said to hell with, you know, competition, commercialism, industrial whatever, to hell with the whole leafy split-level suburban carpool, and went out and lived in a hut.

GEORGE. How'd he make out?

FRANK. I don't know, it's incredibly tedious. But the point is, the point is...my folks *made* me go to college, see. So I go, and they make me read *this* guy, and like Whitman and Kerouac and Hemingway and all these other guys, and they're all saying the same thing: *what are you doing in college?* The only way to learn about life is to go out and *live* it. So I did. About a month ago, I said to hell with it. I dropped out and started living the way man was meant to: armed with nothing but my, like, like, instincts.

GEORGE. Wow. What'd your folks say?

FRANK. Oh pfff – they don't know yet. They mortgaged the house to pay my tuition.

GEORGE. Damn.

Pause. They both sit nodding grimly. Then:

...Well look: I'm gonna do you a favor here, Cochise. I'm gonna put this whole fish thing in proper perspective for you here. You watch this. You ready? This is The Life of a Fish. I'm a fish.

FRANK. You're a fish.

GEORGE. I'm a fish. Here I am, swimmin' around and swimmin' around. Gee, I wonder where the hell I'm goin'? I can't tell, 'cause I got eyes on the sides of my head. There's only right here, right now. No need for memory, no need for worry. When I get where I'm goin', wherever *that* is, I'll forget where I just was, 'cause I'll be someplace else, which is as good as any other, as far as I can see, which ain't *very*, 'cause I got *eyes* on the *sides* of my *head*! Whoa! Look out for that dyke! Watch where you're goin'! – That's a fish joke. Think I'll relieve myself now.

Fart sounds, with bubbles.

Wonder where that went. No way a' knowin'! Think I'll have a few babies now – say, thirty-two.

Birth sounds.

Ah! There! All that works makes me hungry. Think I'll eat the fat ones. Nobody wants fat kids.

He gobbles.

Thanks, kids! Adios! Watch for sharks! – Another fish joke. Hell, where am I now? What difference does it make? None whatsoever. Wait! There's a bit nasty steel hook dressed up as an insect. Didn't one a' them rip out my gums last week? How would I know? Let's have lunch! I haven't eaten anything since beats me.

He chomps.

Mmm! Tastes like nothing I recall! Wait a minute. Whoa! It's fighting back! Where am I going? Who the hell knows? Where have I been? I don't remember!

He flops on the floor for a few seconds, then stops.

…Well, this is interesting. Got one eye on the sky, the other in the mud. Well, enough of this. I'll just swim away.

He flops some more.

…Whew! Musta swum for miles. Whatever that means. Wait! There's a hairy legged fella, wearin' a dress!

He means **FRANK**, *who he looks at with one eye.*

Maybe he knows where I am! Maybe I'll ask him. Ask him what? I don't remember! I don't remember…I don't remem…I don't….

And he 'dies,' with his tongue hanging out. Frank is chuckling, despite himself.

…There. That's how smart a fish is, right there, and I can prove it.

FRANK. How?

GEORGE. I'll make you a bet. I'll bet you I can catch a fish – no, a dozen fish – anytime, anyplace, no matter what your fishics of fizzing horse hockey. I'll bet you ten bucks.

FRANK. Why?

GEORGE. Prostitute Number Four: No fish can outsmart me. Put up or throw up. Deal?

FRANK. Okay! Deal!

GEORGE. Ha! Teach you a thing or two. Francis! Now: Prostitute Number Five: have another beer. Come on, one more, one more, ya pansy, come on, Francis, one more, just one more – (*etc.*).

FRANK. No, no, quit calling me that! Really, no more beer, come on, don't make me do this, no, really, please – (*etc.*).

And so on until blackout. End scene.

Scene 4

In darkness: we hear gunshots in the distance.

At rise: the next morning, still raining. FRANK is asleep on the floor, covered by the afghan. ANNIE, in her night-gown, sits beside him, watching him. ZEE enters from the bedroom, dressed for the day.

ZEE. George? …George?

ANNIE. Ssssshh.

ZEE. …Oh. …What are you – ?

ANNIE. The rain woke me up.

ZEE. How is he?

ANNIE. Seems to have survived.

ZEE. Look at him. He looks so peaceful.

Pause.

…Rise and shine, dear! Time to –

FRANK *groans.*

ANNIE. Mother! Why don't you let him sleep?

ZEE. Too much sleep is unhealthy. He could choke to death on his own saliva. What is that on your face?

ANNIE. Nothing.

ZEE. Are you wearing make-up?

ANNIE. Ts! Noooo!

ZEE. Well go get your robe on. You shouldn't be walking around like that, for heaven's sake. And go yell for your father to come eat.

ANNIE. He won't hear me.

ZEE. (*admiring* **FRANK**) Hmm?

ANNIE. He won't *hear* me. He's out there somewhere. And I dress like this every night.

ZEE. Oh for God's sake, Annie, just go cover up and wash that foolishness off your face.

ANNIE *skulks off to the bedroom.*

Frank? ...Frank dear. Wake up.

FRANK. (*hungover*) Oooooooooooh.

ZEE. Rise and shine, dear. Time to get up.

FRANK. No, no, noooooooo.

ZEE. Wh – what's wrong, dear? Are you injured?

FRANK. My head.

ZEE. What's wrong with it? Did George – did that – did he keep you up all night? I swear I can't turn my back around here for a second. That man is an overgrown fetus. Would you like some coffee?

She helps him to his feet.

FRANK. Coffee. Good. Yes.

ZEE. (*inadvertently yelling in his ear*) Annie!

FRANK. Ooooooh.

ZEE. What's wrong? Is it your leg? Does it hurt?

FRANK. It's a little stiff.

ZEE. Well come over here and sit down. You shouldn't put any weight on it for a few weeks. You could sever an artery. Annie!

Again, right into his ear.

FRANK. Aaaarrh.

ZEE. Poor dear. You're in such pain, aren't you. You can't hide it from me.

One more time:

– *Annnnieeee!* – Put your leg up on this, there you go, just like that. Do you need a pillow? Would you like a sponge bath?

ANNIE *enters from bedroom, dressed or covered up:*

ANNIE. *What!*

ZEE. Run out and get some logs.

ANNIE. It's raining!

ZEE. Don't argue. We need a fire.

ANNIE. But –

ZEE. Hurry up now, don't get wet.

FRANK. Good morning!

> **ANNIE** *smiles at him and exits to the porch and offstage.*

ZEE. Now. How does a nice big breakfast sound?

FRANK. Oh, I don't want you to go to any trouble, ma'am.

ZEE. Some nice, hot blueberry pancakes, smothered in maple syrup, with sausage and wheat toast? I'll bet you haven't had a good meal in weeks.

FRANK. About a month, actually.

ZEE. It's so nice to have you here, Frank. You don't know how wonderful it is. You're like a dream come true. I'm going to take wonderful care of you now.

> **ZEE** *blows him a kiss and exits to the kitchen.*

FRANK. ...Well alright. – Hey, uh, ma'am?

ZEE. (*off*) Yes dear?

FRANK. I'm uh, I'm not so big on pancakes. You got any eggs?

ZEE. (*off*) Fried, scrambled, boiled, poached or Benedict?

FRANK. Scrambled's great. Kinda runny? With cheese?

ZEE. (*off*) Four eggs or five?

FRANK. Wow. Uh – five! Got any bell pepper?

ZEE. (*off*) Coming right up, dear.

FRANK. ...Well alright.

> **ANNIE** *enters, carrying an armload of logs, most of which she drops as she enters.* **FRANK** *rises to help her.*

ZEE. (*off*) George, is that you?

FRANK. (*because she won't answer*) ...It's uh...it's Annie.

ZEE. (*off*) You're not wet are you Annie?

> **ANNIE** *rolls her eyes but won't answer.*

FRANK. Uh, no ma'am.

Pause. To **ANNIE***:*

...Hi. I'm uh –

ZEE. (*off*) Would you like some juice, Robbie?

FRANK. What'd she – ?

ANNIE. She meant Frank.

FRANK. Uh – yes please! – Is there something...?

ZEE. (*off*) Orange, apple or grape?

FRANK. Orange is fine! – Are you okay?

ZEE. (*off*) Jam on your toast?

FRANK. Sounds great! – Are you mad about something?

ZEE. (*off*) Apricot, strawberry or mixed fruit?

FRANK. *Mixed fruit!*

ANNIE. It's not you.

Gunshots are heard in the distance. **ZEE** *rushes in.*

ZEE. What is that lunatic doing?

ANNIE. Who knows.

ZEE. Well I'm not holding his breakfast for him. He can just starve to death for all I care.

FRANK. You want me to go look for him?

ZEE. In your condition? Don't be ridiculous. You could open that wound and get maggots. Besides, I haven't fixed your pants yet.

ANNIE. I can do that.

ZEE. I'll do it. You just go dry yourself off. I told you not to get wet.

ZEE exits back to the kitchen. **ANNIE** *takes a towel from the chest or somewhere and dries her hair.*

FRANK. ...How old are you?

ANNIE. Why.

FRANK. Because your mother doesn't seem to know.

ANNIE. She doesn't like anyone to grow up. That's why she married my dad. He's twelve.

FRANK. He's a great guy. They both are. You're really lucky.

ANNIE. Huh.

FRANK. You are. You got, like, the whole family thing here.

ANNIE. Not quite.

FRANK. My family's all screwed up. My dad free-bases anti-depressants, and who can blame him. He's a proctologist. I can hardly bring myself to shake his hand. And my mom, she's like the most un-spiritual person I know. She –

ANNIE. She's a crazed shop-a-holic. She consumes everything and creates nothing. Except for a hole in the ozone that follows her around in her SUV.

FRANK. ...You heard.

ANNIE. You've dated two slutty cheerleaders and a gymnast and once saw your best friend's mother's boob. When you were on the swim team, you shaved your whole body and went commando for a week. Once, when your folks were out of town –

FRANK. You *listened.*

ANNIE. It was pretty entertaining until you passed out and he went running out into the rain.

FRANK. Who covered me up?

ANNIE smiles – and he catches on, then abruptly drops the log he's been holding.

FRANK. Ow!

ANNIE. What.

FRANK. Splinter.

ANNIE. Let me see.

She takes his hand and looks at it. He looks at her.

FRANK. ...So how old are you?

ANNIE. ...How old do you think?

FRANK. I don't know, like...twenty three?

ANNIE. Riiiight.

FRANK. Well that's what I first thought. I was like, "thank you God."

ANNIE. Riiight.

FRANK. I was. I swear. ...I'm serious.

Pause. She gets a needle to work on his splinter.

ANNIE. ...So what's it like?

FRANK. What's what like?

ANNIE. ...You know. Being out. On your own.

FRANK. Why?

ANNIE. ...I don't know.

FRANK. It's uh....you know. Great. Master of your fate, all that. It's exciting, like the first time you ran away from home, before the scary part.

ANNIE. I've never run away from home.

FRANK. Or stayed out late. Or snuck out your window. Or snuck somebody in.

ANNIE. I never did any of that. I can't do anything without my mother reminding me what a good girl I am. "You're our angel, Annie, our blessed little angel."

FRANK. That sucks.

ANNIE. Big time.

She sucks/gnaws on his finger to get to the splinter.

FRANK. ...Um. I could show you.

ANNIE. Show me what.

FRANK. The world. I've seen it. I could show it to you.

She stops sucking and looks at him.

...Whenever you're ready. Whenever you decide to say to hell with it.

ANNIE. (*contemplating – with sadistic glee*) ...It'd *kill* 'em.

FRANK. They'd get over it. ...Okay so, how old are you really?

ANNIE. ...I don't know. They won't tell me.

She removes the splinter with the needle.

There. You're healed.

FRANK. My mom used to kiss it better.

ANNIE pauses, then takes his hand and kisses it nervously. He touches her cheek. They gaze into each other's eyes. An intimacy is about to develop when – BOOM! The door flies open and GEORGE bursts into the room. He is soaking wet, in his stocking feet, and carries two rubber boots and a shotgun.

GEORGE. Yee haw! He's back! They said he couldn't do it, but here he is, and he's got a surprise!

ZEE enters from kitchen.

ZEE. George! Where have you been!

GEORGE. Fishing!

He empties the boots onto the rug; they're loaded with bloody fish.

Whatever you're burning in there, take it off! I want these babies cleaned and scaled.

– Franky boy, pay the man!

ZEE. Where did you get these?

GEORGE. Where do you think I got 'em? The river! It's full of 'em!

ZEE. You don't even have a pole!

GEORGE. Don't need no pole!

ANNIE. They're all...bloody!

FRANK. How did you catch them?

GEORGE. Don't matter how I caught 'em! I won the bet! – Bet Hot Shot here ten bucks I could catch a dozen fish before feeding time, which it is, right now, for us.

ANNIE. They're deformed!

GEORGE. They're not deformed! Just got a little lead in 'em!

ANNIE. They're full of bullets!

GEORGE. It's buckshot!

FRANK. You *shot* them?

GEORGE. No, I didn't *shoot* them. Not *at* them. I shot *around* them. You should have seen it! It was beautiful! I find

all the big rocks – like you said – where I figure they're
all huddled up? *Blam*! Flashes of silver in the sky!

ZEE. George, they're mutilated!

GEORGE. Just get the lead out. Use a magnet or something.

FRANK. You didn't even try to fish for them!

GEORGE. I did it my way! Pay the man!

ZEE. Don't you give him a cent!

ANNIE. Look at them! They're –

GEORGE. Just cut it out, you two! This is between him and
me. You just go cook 'em up.

ZEE. We won't touch them!

ANNIE. (*smelling trouble*) Mama –

GEORGE. You'll do as I say. I'm still the boss around here.

ANNIE. I'll do it. I'll clean them.

ZEE. You will not! I won't allow it!

GEORGE. You won't *what*? You won't *allow* it?

ANNIE. Daddy, wait.

GEORGE. What are you, the Permission Lady?

ZEE. Come on, Frank. Your eggs are done.

> **ZEE** *pulls* **FRANK** *away, but* **GEORGE** *grabs his other
> arm: a tug- of-war.*

GEORGE. We're not having eggs! We're having fish!

ZEE. Release this boy, you –

GEORGE. Hag!

ZEE. Baboon!

GEORGE. Giant nipple!

> **ZEE** *gasps.*

ANNIE. Stop it, stop it, stop it!

GEORGE. Are you his mother? – Is she your mother? Did
she adopt you while I was gone?

ZEE. I'm warning you, George!

> **ZEE** *and* **GEORGE** *square off, eye-to-eye, except that*

FRANK *is between them.*

GEORGE. Damn you, old woman. You'd think you'd have learned by now. Just leave him be! Get your hooks out of him, 'cause he ain't yours. Got it? ...Now there's the kitchen. Those are breakfast? Get it?

Pause. A standoff. Then, ZEE *suddenly smiles, backs down, and picks up the rug full of fish.*

ZEE. ...Oh yes, George. I get it now. It's all verrrry clear.

ZEE *exits to kitchen.* ANNIE *is seething.*

GEORGE. ...You got something to say, Bucky?

ANNIE. ...Yeah! ...To hell with it!

ANNIE *storms off to the bedroom. Pause.*

GEORGE. (*happily*) ...Women!

FRANK. What was all that about?

GEORGE. Just a little household maintenance. Nothin' to worry about. – Somebody! Beer! *Now*!

This last he shouts into the kitchen.

We're gonna have us a fish fry, Franky boy! Have us some fun.

FRANK. You can't eat that fish!

GEORGE. Might be a little crunchy, but –

FRANK. No, no, you missed the whole point, George! You don't go out and *destroy*! It's man and nature, co-existing –

GEORGE. I could catch more fish with my *fists* than you could with that – *fly thing of yours.*

FRANK. Look.

GEORGE. I could catch more fish with my *teeth.* I'll *bet* you.

FRANK. Knock it off, George!

GEORGE. Mr. Man in Nature. I'll bet you, and if I win...you have to stay here and go fishing with me for a week.

FRANK. ...What if I win?

GEORGE. If you win...I go fishing with you. ...I could use

the company, tell you the truth. Figure you could too, you know?

ZEE *enters with a creepily polite smile and two cans of beer, which she sets on the table, and then exits.*

...So what do you say?

FRANK *watches* ZEE *go, then looks off in the direction Annie went.*

FRANK. ...Deal.

GEORGE. Beer?

FRANK. Beer.

They open the beers, which spray all over.

GEORGE. (*yelling off*) That's very funny, Zee. I'm not cleaning it up.

The two get comfortable on the couch.

...Well alright. Here we are. Tell you what, Franky boy. This is the kind of thing I been missin'. Cheers.

FRANK. Cheers.

GEORGE. You're a helluva guy, you know that?

FRANK. Thanks.

GEORGE. 'Bout time I told you that. And it's good to have a friend, you know? ...Friends.

FRANK. Friends.

GEORGE. That's right. A helluva guy. ...I'll bet your daddy's mighty proud of you.

FRANK. I'll bet he won't be.

GEORGE. Ehhh. I'd be proud of you. Maybe you two – maybe you two just need to...sit down and...talk it out, you know?

FRANK. Maybe not.

GEORGE. You should though. You should talk to each other, as much as you can. 'Cause... father and son, you know? That's sacred. It's a sacred thing. ...Wish I could tell him that.

FRANK. Who?

GEORGE. My uh…uh, my….

> **GEORGE** *slips into a haze, lost in something. Then he snaps himself back out.*

…Well, what's done is done. Ain't gonna sit around feelin' sorry for myself. I mean, that's life, ain't it? Hard road that knows no turning. 'What *my* daddy used to say. A hard road that knows no turning. Big, loud son of a gun, my daddy.

FRANK. Really.

GEORGE. Big Bob, they called him. Used to take me to the Broken Butt Saloon every Tuesday and Friday night after my mama left. Get us both drunk, chase around them bar girls. Lord, he loved to fight. I'd be leanin' over the pool table or somethin', and – *bam!* We'd roll around the floor and crash into somebody and he'd get me in a headlock and throw me across the room. Got us both arrested once. Broke that finger twice.

FRANK. …*Why?*

GEORGE. …It's a hard road, Franky boy. Guess it was his way of makin' sure I'd be ready.

> **GEORGE** *gets wistful again.* **FRANK** *is appalled.*

…Yup. Father and son. Sacred. It's a sacred bond.

FRANK. Mmm.

GEORGE. Otherwise, what've you got? Without that, you know? What do you do? …Right through the rail and over the edge. You know? …It happens.

FRANK. …What happens.

GEORGE. That. Happened to…happened to a friend of mine.

FRANK. …What did?

GEORGE. …I don't know. Lost control. …That's what they…. I don't know, though. I just…I don't know.

> **GEORGE** *is back in his fog. Long pause.*

FRANK. ...You alright, George?

GEORGE. Hmm? ...Me? Hell yeah! You ready?

FRANK. Ready for what?

GEORGE. Fishing! What, you forget already?

FRANK. ...Now? It's *raining.*

GEORGE. Ah, it ain't hardly even sprinkling.

FRANK. Yes it is, it's —

GEORGE. Here's the rules. You do it your way, with your little "mosquito" there, and I'll do it grizzly style. Man in nature.

FRANK. You weren't serio —

GEORGE. Catch as many as you can, and meet back here at —

FRANK. George, it's — !

GEORGE. High noon! Latecomers disqualified! Wanna double the bet? So if I win, we stay up here two weeks?

FRANK. It's a *downpour* out there!

GEORGE. I'll throw in my daughter.

FRANK. ...What?

GEORGE. I saw the way you been lookin' at her. She ain't ugly. A little stubborn, kinda moody. Got a hell of a mouth on her though.

FRANK. ...Deal!

GEORGE. Deal! Hot dog! I'll see you at the showdown!

FRANK. Okay!

GEORGE. Okay! Okay!

> **GEORGE** *grabs his rubber boots and "okays" all the way out the front door and off the porch.*

FRANK. Wait! I don't...I don't have any pants! ...Or shoes. Or a fishing pole.

> **ANNIE** *has entered from the bedroom, dressed, with a bag or pack. During the following she rounds up his coat, shoes and pack and hands them to him.*

ANNIE. Not that that would make any difference.

FRANK. True. This is working out great! Two weeks fishing, all the comforts of home. Good company.

ANNIE. You enjoy the attention.

FRANK. …Are you mad at me again?

ANNIE. I told you, it's not you. Let's go.

FRANK. Go? Go where?

ANNIE. I'm taking you up on your offer. Let's get out of here.

FRANK. What, leave? Now?

ANNIE. Yup.

FRANK. You people have no sense of occasion.

ANNIE. Do you want to stay here for the rest of your life?

FRANK. …Well.

ANNIE. Forget it.

She starts off.

FRANK. Annie, you can't just –

ANNIE. Don't! Tell me what I can't do! I know what I can't do! I can't live with them anymore. I can't even live with myself.

FRANK. What are you talking about?

ANNIE. You don't know what's going on here, and I don't have time to explain. Either come with me, or get out of the way.

FRANK. You know, you're really putting me in –

She kisses him hard. He's convinced.

…Well okay.

He grabs his coat, pack and shoes, and stands there, without pants and in his stocking feet, ready to go.

Seems like just a few minutes ago, my life was really shaping up, you know? Seems like I finally caught a break. But – what the hell! I'm an idiot. Got my pack. Got my coat. Got no idea what I'm doing. Are you sure this is what you want?

ANNIE *nods.*

…Okay. Let's go.

And they head out onto the porch. **FRANK** *realizes:*

Wait! My pants!

ANNIE. I'll find them. Go ahead. I'll catch up.

FRANK. But!

ANNIE. There's a bait shop up on the highway. I'll meet you there.

FRANK exits; ANNIE enters the house and starts looking around for the pants. ZEE calls from the kitchen:

ZEE. (*off*) …Annie?

ANNIE. Crap!

ZEE. Annie? Is that you?

ANNIE hides her pack in the hope chest. ZEE enters.

ANNIE. Yup.

ZEE. I thought I heard the door.

ANNIE. That was…me. I was out…looking for wood.

ZEE. We have wood.

ANNIE. It's wet. I was looking for…dry wood.

ZEE. Where are the boys?

ANNIE. Uh. Fishing.

ZEE. Fishing? I haven't even fixed Robbie's pants yet!

ANNIE. Frank's. Where are they?

ZEE. It's pouring rain out there! He'll catch cold and his lungs will collapse.

ANNIE. Good point. I'll go get him.

ZEE. No, you'll catch one too. Besides, you're going to help me with those fish.

ZEE laughs and tows ANNIE off toward the kitchen.

ANNIE. No, but, but…help you *what?*

ZEE. I'm not sure yet. But if it's fish he wants, it's fish he's gonna get! Ahahahaha!

ANNIE *looks back toward the door as she's towed offstage.*

End Act I.

ACT TWO

At rise: later that morning. Outside, it's still raining. Inside, ZEE *is supervising* ANNIE, *who is sitting on the couch knitting the afghan.*

ZEE. ...Don't be in such a hurry, Annie. It's too tight again.

ANNIE. Why are we even doing this? Why can't we just take it out and throw –

ZEE. Why are you so jumpy? You act like you can't wait to –

ANNIE. I can't fix it, Mother! No one can! Why can't we just accept that and, and –

ZEE. Try, Annie. Do it for Robbie.

ANNIE. His name is Frank, Mother.

ZEE. I *meant* Robbie. Do it for him.

ANNIE. How will Robbie –

ZEE. Do it for me, then. Please? I don't know why, but... please?

ANNIE. ...Alright.

ZEE. ...You've been such a blessing, Annie, through all of this. I just don't know what we'd have done without you. ...You're an angel, you know. Our own angel.

ZEE exits to kitchen. ANNIE *sighs, thinks for a second, stands, and looks back and forth between the kitchen and the front door.*

She starts to gather her pack from the chest, but GEORGE *enters from outside, wet and subdued. He stands. Pause.*

GEORGE. ...Well?

ANNIE. Well what.

GEORGE. I'm back.

ANNIE. That's great.

GEORGE. How come there ain't a fire?

ANNIE. The wood is all wet.

GEORGE. How did it get wet?

ANNIE. Nobody's really sure.

> **ZEE** *calls from off:*

ZEE. (*off*) Annie, did I hear the door?

ANNIE. It's Daddy.

ZEE. (*off*) Oooh, good. Welcome home, dear! I'll be out in one minute.

> **GEORGE** *is stupefied by her tone.*

GEORGE. Where's what's-his-name?

ANNIE. Frank. Beats me.

GEORGE. He ain't here yet?

ANNIE. Nope.

GEORGE. Yee-haw! Disqualification! The winnah! I win the bet!

ZEE. (*off*) What bet is that, dear?

GEORGE. I ain't telling you.

ANNIE. Daddy won Frank in a bet.

ZEE. (*off*) Really?

GEORGE. Damn right.

ZEE. (*off*) Did you catch any more fish?

GEORGE. I ain't tellin' you.

ANNIE. No.

GEORGE. Yes! I caught one! ...See?

> *He takes a minnow from his shirt pocket.*

ANNIE. Must've put up quite a fight.

GEORGE. I found him. Down on the trail by the river. Just lyin' there, flappin' his gills in the rain. Don't know how he got there.

ANNIE. Maybe you blasted him up there this morning.

GEORGE. I didn't know what to do with him. So I picked him up and held him in my hand and just sorta... watched him. He kept hangin' on and hangin' on.... So finally I just bashed his head in with a rock. You can cook him up if you want.

ANNIE. Mom saved the eggs. They've been waiting for hours.

GEORGE. What's wrong with you, Bucko?

ANNIE. Nothing.

GEORGE. Female trouble?

ANNIE. Noooo! ...It's Mother.

GEORGE. That's what I meant.

He tousles her hair; she smiles despite herself.

Women have this gland, see. If they don't bitch, it explodes, and they die. That's why us guys gotta periodically leave the toilet seat up. Right? Huh? Huh?

ANNIE *allows herself a chuckle.* **ZEE** *enters with a cup of coffee.*

ZEE. Here's some nice, hot coffee for you, dear.

GEORGE. Who, me?

ZEE. Of course, you. And I put it in your favorite Star Trek Travel Mug, with the lid, so you don't spill and burn yourself.

GEORGE. What the hell's goin' on here?

ZEE. What do you mean?

GEORGE. I mean, what the hell's goin' on here? You're bein' nice to me.

ZEE. Oh, go ahead. Take it. I made it special, just for you.

GEORGE. ...Well I, I guess I oughta...guess I oughta apologize for...yellin' at ya like I did, huh?

ZEE. Thank you dear. That's very nice.

GEORGE. I don't mean most of the stuff I say to you, you know.

ZEE. I know. Drink your coffee.

GEORGE. And shootin' the quilt there, I'm sorry about that.

ZEE. It's an afghan.

GEORGE. Except that was kinda funny.

ZEE. It was a scream, dear. Drink your coffee.

GEORGE. You two never could stay mad at me for too long. Ain't that right, Bucky?

ANNIE. Drink your coffee.

GEORGE. What say this family has some breakfast!

> **GEORGE** *still has not drunk his coffee.*

ZEE. We can't eat without Robbie.

GEORGE. *Bob.*

ANNIE. Frank!

GEORGE. I'll go find him. He probably hasn't caught any yet, and he's too proud to give up. He's got grit, that boy.

ANNIE. Maybe he left.

> *They look blankly at her.*

...I mean, maybe he found a ride out or something.

ZEE. Well, he wouldn't just...just leave without saying good-bye!

GEORGE. Where would he go?

ZEE. He's got nowhere to go. I think he's an orphan.

ANNIE. He's not an –

ZEE. My god! What if he got struck by lightning!

ANNIE. He wasn't struck by –

GEORGE. I better go find him.

ZEE. Hurry George! Go!

GEORGE. Okay! Hold your eggs!

> **GEORGE** *hands the cup and the minnow to* **ZEE** *and runs out the door.*

ZEE. Wait! You forgot your...! Rats.

> **ZEE** *shrugs, lifts the lid on the cup, and drops the*

minnow into the coffee. Pause.

ANNIE. ...Mama? ...He's gone.

ZEE. We'll find him, sweetheart.

ANNIE. No Mama. Listen. He's gone.... He had to go. It's too late.

ZEE. How do you...how do you know that?

ANNIE. He didn't know how to tell you, so...he just left.

ZEE. He could hardly walk! He wasn't ready to –

ANNIE. I know! I told him!

ZEE. Why did he go? Was it something...did we...did I do something or – ?

ANNIE. No, Mama, it wasn't you.

ZEE. Why didn't you make him stay?

ANNIE. I tried, I...tried, Mama, but –

ZEE. You're not telling something. You're hiding something behind your back.

ANNIE. No.

ZEE. You spiteful, selfish little –

ANNIE. It's not my fault!

ZEE. I'd like to know what you did to make him run off like that!

ANNIE. I didn't do anything! Why can't he just go if that's what he wants? God, this family is like a prison!

ZEE. Oh is that so? Well maybe you should have just gone with him, if that's how you –

ANNIE. Maybe I should have!

ZEE. Well what kept you? Just go, if that's what you want! I don't know what we did that was so terrible. All we ever tried to do was help!

ANNIE. I know, Mama.

ZEE. But if you don't need us –

ANNIE. Mama!

ZEE. We don't need you either! We don't need you!

ANNIE. Mama!

ANNIE *reaches for* **ZEE,** *but* **ZEE** *recoils. Then: boom!*
GEORGE *bursts through the front door, half-dragging*
FRANK, *who is unconscious.*

GEORGE. I found him! I found him! Right down the hill,
by the river!

ANNIE. Frank?

ZEE. Oh dear! Frank? Frank dear? – Set him in a chair. No,
put him on the couch. – Annie, go get some towels.

ANNIE. Frank?

ZEE. Hurry, Annie!

ANNIE *runs off to the kitchen.* **ZEE** *removes his coat, etc.*

GEORGE. He was passed out on the riverbank. He must
have fallen in the river. I shook him as hard as I could
but he wouldn't wake up.

ZEE. He's soaked to the skin! Quick! Get a fire going!

ANNIE *enters from kitchen with a towel.*

ANNIE. Here's a towel. And I put some hot water on. Is he
awake?

ZEE. He's in a coma or something. And his leg is bleeding!
God, if gangrene sets in I'll never forgive myself.

GEORGE *is at the fireplace, trying to get a fire started.*

GEORGE. This wood's all wet!

ZEE. (*to* **ANNIE**) Go get some bandages.

GEORGE. This won't burn!

ZEE. And put some hot water on.

ANNIE. I did!

GEORGE. Ow. Splinter!

ANNIE *exits to kitchen.*

ZEE. And get some alcohol.

GEORGE. And some gasoline.

ANNIE. (*off*) I can't find any alcohol.

ZEE. Then get a beer!

GEORGE. Make that two!

ANNIE enters empty-handed.

ANNIE. We used all the bandages last night.
ZEE. Look in that chest.

GEORGE picks up the afghan. ANNIE opens the chest.

GEORGE. Here's a blanket!
ZEE. It's an afghan, George!

She takes it and covers FRANK, tucking him in.

Robbie? Robbie? Wake up son. What day is this? Can you tell me? Do you know your name?
GEORGE. Wake up, son! Snap out of it!

ZEE gently slaps him.

ZEE. Give us a sign, anything!
GEORGE. Hit him harder. Harder!
ZEE. Robbie! Robbie! Rise and shine! Rise and shine! – Annie, where are those bandages?

ANNIE has been standing at the hope chest, clutching the pack she hid there, looking at them. Now she hides the pack in the chest again.

ANNIE. Uh…I can't find any.
GEORGE. There's a Ranger Rick first aid kit in the car!
ZEE. Go George! Go! – Annie, take over here. I'll find some alcohol.

GEORGE bounds out the front door and off. ZEE runs into the kitchen. ANNIE is left alone with FRANK.

ANNIE. …Oh, God! I'm sorry! …I didn't mean for this to happen. I didn't think – I thought you'd made it. I really thought you'd made it.

FRANK opens his eyes and sits up.

FRANK. Where the hell were you?

ANNIE shrieks and jumps back.

I waited for like an hour.

ANNIE. You! You were –

FRANK. Faking.

ANNIE. You – !

She hits him.

FRANK. Ow!

ANNIE. I got held up! She caught me.

ZEE. (*off*) Annie?

> **ANNIE** *pushes* **FRANK** *back down. He is "unconscious" again as* **ZEE** *enters.*

Annie, where is the alcohol?

ANNIE. He's coming around, mother! – Wake up, Frank! Wake up!

She belts him. **GEORGE** *hurdles in with a first aid kit.*

FRANK. Oooooooh.

GEORGE. Here's the first aid kit.

ZEE. He's coming around! – Wake up, son! Wake up!

FRANK. Huh? Huh? …Where am I?

GEORGE. You're here!

ZEE. It's us! You're home!

GEORGE. I saved you! Just in time!

> **FRANK** *gropes for their faces.*

FRANK. …Mom? …Dad?

ZEE. Yes! Yes! – He's in a daze.

FRANK. Oh thank God!

ZEE. Annie, go get the eggs.

FRANK. There's no place like home! There's no place like home!

ZEE. There there, son, you're alright now. I've got you. – Annie?

> **ANNIE** *is looking on angrily.*

GEORGE. I'll get 'em.

> **GEORGE** *runs off to kitchen.*

FRANK. Annie! Sis! It's you!

> **ANNIE** *throws a towel in his face and runs off to her bedroom.* **GEORGE** *enters with a plateful of eggs.*

GEORGE. What's wrong with her?

ZEE. Who knows. Here – give me those!

> **ZEE** *takes the eggs; she and* **GEORGE** *sit on the couch on either side of* **FRANK.**

GEORGE. Well, scoot over, Zee, you're crowding him!

ZEE. You scoot over. I'm feeding him. We've got to keep his strength up.

FRANK. Annie?

> *As he calls to* **ANNIE, ZEE** *stuffs eggs into his mouth.*

GEORGE. Well let him talk if he wants to talk.

ZEE. What's wrong, dear?

FRANK. The eggs, ma'am. They're…they're –

> **GEORGE** *grabs the coffee cup.*

GEORGE. Here, wash 'em down with some coffee!

ZEE. Don't give him that!

> *Too late.* **FRANK** *drinks the coffee and immediately spits it out.*

FRANK. Eaaaaakkkk!

GEORGE. What's wrong?

FRANK. It's *horrible*!

ZEE. Give me that!

> *But* **GEORGE** *has taken the cup and now looks inside.*

GEORGE. Well there's a fish head floatin' around in there!

> **FRANK** *gags and glops his tongue.*

There's a whole *bunch* of fish heads floatin' around in

there!

ZEE. George, will you let me handle this!

GEORGE. Well not if you're going to poison him!

FRANK stands and calls:

FRANK. *Annie!*

ZEE pulls him back down.

ZEE. You sit down!

GEORGE. Take it easy on him already!

ZEE. I'm not done putting him back together yet!

She grabs the first aid kit.

GEORGE. Well we got a business proposition to work out, ain't that right, Franky boy?

ZEE. Not now, George!

GEORGE. And you remember the stakes, right Franky boy?

ZEE. Does this hurt?

She pokes at his wounds. FRANK is groaning and nodding at them both.

GEORGE. And you agreed like a gentleman, ain't that right, Franky boy?

ZEE. How about this?

FRANK stands.

FRANK. Aaaaaaggghh!

GEORGE. Shake!

ZEE. Sit!

A vertical tug-o-war as GEORGE shakes his hand while ZEE tries to pull him back down.

FRANK. Annie! Help!

GEORGE AND ZEE. (*simultaneously, to one another*) Would you leave him alone!

FRANK. Annie!

ZEE. Annie's gone. You can't see her.

GEORGE. Why not?

ZEE. Because I say so.

GEORGE. Bucky!

>**GEORGE** *heads off toward the bedrooms.*

ZEE. George! You just leave her be!

GEORGE. (*off*) Come on in here, little girl. Put that down. No no, put it down. You come in here with me. Franky boy wants to see you.

ZEE. George! All she wants is attention! George! – Dammit! You – just sit! – George!

>**ZEE** *starts off toward the bedroom, but meets* **GEORGE** *coming in, with* **ANNIE** *in tow.*

GEORGE. Come on, Bucky. Sit down over here.

ZEE. No! I forbid it! Put her back, George!

GEORGE. You two excuse us.

ZEE. Annie!

GEORGE. Pay no attention to the screaming.

>**GEORGE** *tows* **ZEE** *off to the kitchen. Long pause as we hear the sound of a great battle – pots and pans and such – in the kitchen. Then quiet.*

FRANK. …*Now* you're mad at me.

ANNIE. Yup.

FRANK. Why? What have I –

ANNIE. You think this is funny.

FRANK. …Yeah, kinda.

ANNIE. You let yourself get caught.

FRANK. No, I –

ANNIE. And you pretended to be hurt so –

FRANK. I *am* hurt! Look! Blood!

ANNIE. – so he would drag you back here, and you pretended to be unconscious so they –

FRANK. It seemed like the thing –

ANNIE. – would shower you with attention. Well you better get used to it, because they've got you now!

FRANK. I didn't know where you were! What was I supposed to do?

ANNIE. You were supposed to wait for me!

FRANK. I did wait for you! I stood around in the bait shop, trying on hats, in my *underwear*. Until finally I thought, wait! Maybe she's in trouble! Maybe she needs me! So I came back down the trail, in my *underwear*, lightning flashing all around me, water up to here – and I... slipped on a rock and –

ANNIE. And fell in the river.

FRANK. ...This isn't funny.

ANNIE. I know.

FRANK. I could have been killed!

ANNIE. Does it hurt?

FRANK. Yeah it hurts! It hurts a lot!

ANNIE. Sit down.

FRANK. No.

ANNIE. Sit down. Please? I'm sorry. I'm sorry you fell in the river again.

She begins to bandage his leg.

FRANK. It had me this time, I swear. I tried to swim, I tried to fight it, but I kept going under and going under, until everything started going...kinda blurry.

ANNIE. (*smiling*) Mmmm.

FRANK. And I had this...this vision.

ANNIE. Vision.

FRANK. Yeah. It was like I was a kid, and we were at the beach, me and my folks. I could see them standing there, on the shore, waving.

ANNIE. Waving.

FRANK. Yeah. And I was way out in the ocean, waving at them, harder and harder. And they were waving back. They didn't understand, though. I'd swum out too far. I was trying to tell them – warn them – I couldn't get back in! ...But they thought I was waving. So we kept... waving at each other, and all the while, I was going farther and farther away....

ANNIE. ...So what happened?

FRANK. That's all I remember. Next thing I know your father's got me by the armpits trying to shake my head off.

ANNIE. Jees.

FRANK. What could I tell him? I was running away? I figured I'd better talk to you first, get the story straight. So –

ANNIE. So you played dead.

FRANK. Not bad, huh?

ANNIE. And if I wasn't here? What if I'd already left? What would you do then?

FRANK. Hope they didn't bury me too deep.

ANNIE smiles. So does FRANK. He reaches out and touches her cheek. She allows it, maybe even takes his hand.

...Speaking of which, I think there's a dead poodle out by your woodpile.

ANNIE. ...It's kind of hard to explain.

They smile. A nice moment. He's about to move in for a kiss, when ZEE enters and blows the whole thing:

ZEE. Annie!

ANNIE. Mama!

ZEE. George! George!

GEORGE. (*still off*) What!

ANNIE runs off to her bedroom. ZEE follows closely behind.

ZEE. Annie! Annie!

ZEE exits. Pause. FRANK stands alone, feeling awkward. GEORGE limps in from the kitchen with an ice pack on his head.

GEORGE. ...You know, the mood swings around here'll just about kill ya.

End scene.

Scene 2

In darkness: we hear **ZEE** *softly calling, onstage, "Robbie? Robbie?"*

At rise: late at night and still raining. **FRANK** *is sleeping on the couch, huddled under the blanket. He is dreaming uneasily, mumbling things.* **ZEE,** *in her robe, has stolen in from the bedroom. She's holding a pillow and calling to him dreamily.*

ZEE. ...Robbie? ...Robbie? ...Oh. Frank. Are you awake? Would you like some cocoa? ...Oh, you're dreaming. Good. You sleep.

She exits to the kitchen, humming, and enters again with a bowl of bloody fish parts. She sits on the couch by **FRANK**'s *feet. He mumbles, sniffs.*

Sssssh.

She sings:

"Hushaby...don't you cry...go to sleep, my little baby. When you wake...you shall have...all the pretty little ponies." Do you remember that?

FRANK *hums happily in his sleep.* **ZEE** *extracts the pillow from the pillow case.*

Want to hear a story? I have a new one. Once upon a time...a very, very dark time...in a dreary little cabin in the woods, there lived an ogre.

She drops a fish into the pillow case.

Who loved fish.

Another.

Couldn't get enough.

Another. **FRANK** *mumbles something about fish.*

Ssssh.

She hums the song.

…You remind me of someone, have I told you that? He was a beautiful…beautiful boy. Just a boy, he….

Pause. She collects herself.

…Well, anyway – everyday the ogre would go out, shooting and destroying all the creatures in the forest. And every night he returned to terrorize his family. His wife conspired to kill him. But she was too good a person to go through with it.

More fish into the pillowcase.

…But one night their…boy ran away. Never even said…goodbye. They say he had an accident. …I don't know why he…where he was going. He didn't say. He never even said….

Pause. She is almost weeping.

…So every night, his mother lies awake, listening for him. "Goodbye mama, I love you." "Goodbye my baby. God bless you. Goodbye."

Pause. She smiles sadly – then dumps the rest of the fish into the pillowcase.

…And all the while the ogre sleeps beside her, curled up tightly, clutching his pillow.

She exits to the bedroom with the pillowcase full of fish. **FRANK** *remains fast asleep.*

End scene.

Scene 3

In darkness: we hear **ANNIE**'s *voice, softly calling,* "Frank? Frank?"

At rise: later that night. **FRANK** *is still asleep under the blanket.* **ANNIE** *stands over him. She bends and kisses his cheek.*

ANNIE. (*softly, fondly*) Frank. Wake up. ...Frank. Frank?

No response. She pounds the couch.

Frank!

FRANK. Huh? Oh....Annie. ...What time is it?

ANNIE. A few hours to sunrise. Get up, we're leaving.

FRANK. ...Man, this is really getting old.

ANNIE. Come on. It's now or never.

FRANK. Can't do it. Can't go out there again.

ANNIE. I need to do this before I change my mind.

FRANK. Change your mind.

ANNIE. Frank! Don't make this harder than it already is. You don't understand the situation.

FRANK. Me? *Me?* I don't think *you* understand the situation. There's all kinds of things you people aren't quite *grasping* around here:

(A): I am *naked.* I've spent a lot of time naked in this place. I have no secrets and no dignity here. I think I'm getting a cold, but if your mother finds out, I'll never get my pants back and I'll die of exposure.

(B): I am *wounded.* My leg hurts. If I go skipping into the river and through the woods again, it'll get infected and fall off!

ANNIE. Shhh!

FRANK. (C): I'm hungry. I haven't eaten much lately, and what I have eaten has made me want to hurl, which I'd do if I had the strength, which I don't because I've spent most of my time in a torrential rainstorm out that door!

(D): There is a torrential rainstorm out that door! It's pretty hard to miss, but so far everybody has. It's paralyzing the mountainside and seems bent on destroying everything. A step out that door is suicide! Granted, it's no picnic in here either. Between Florence Nightingale and Ranger Rick in there, I've been captured, searched, stripped, tied up, interrogated, intoxicated, captured again, stripped again, poisoned, pushed, pulled and pretty much parented to within an inch of my life! And *that, that,* is the situation!

ANNIE *kicks him in the leg.*

Ah! Ow! What'd you do that for?

ANNIE. Just move. I'm leaving.

FRANK. You want to tell me what's going on around here?

ANNIE. You wouldn't understand, and you wouldn't care.

FRANK. Does it have something to do with Robbie?

ANNIE. ...Wh – ?

FRANK. Robbie! Robbie! It's like there's another person here. I keep looking around for him. Who is Robbie?

ANNIE. He's my...he's my brother. He's....

FRANK. He's dead.

ANNIE *nods.*

...I'm sorry.

ANNIE *shrugs.*

...How did. What –

ANNIE. One morning. Just at sunrise. We got a call. He'd... he'd snuck out that night, taken my father's truck. He –

FRANK. (*it dawns on him*) He had an accident. He missed a curve or lost control and...drove through a rail.... Your father told me, but I didn't realize it.

ANNIE. I don't know if it was an accident.

FRANK. ...You mean –

ANNIE. I don't know! ...There was something wrong with

Robbie. ...If I didn't stand with him every day on the playground, he would have been all alone. If I didn't pick him for kickball, nobody would have. It was like that his whole life. Daddy tried to teach him, he'd take him to games, they'd play catch in the yard, and when Robbie got beat up he'd have to *hide* because if Daddy found out he'd *drag* him out to the garage and try to... he'd *make* him, they'd.... And Mama screaming, "you leave him *alone!*" They'd *fight* over him like that...and Robbie would...

FRANK. ...What.

ANNIE. ...I don't know. ...I just know we can't live with each other anymore. Mama, she can't sleep, she wanders the house at night. Daddy won't talk about it, he rented this place so we could...hide out and...just pretend it never happened. But we keep running into him. We can't seem to get rid of him. You're wearing his shirt.

FRANK. Did he have any pants?

Pause. ANNIE *smiles sadly.*

Well, at least now I know why you wanted me out of here.

ANNIE. You? No. No I don't want –

FRANK. It's alright, Annie. I understand. Tomorrow morning, I'll get up, have a nice cup of fish head coffee – no, no, listen – and I'll give it to 'em straight. Goodbye, it's been great, may I please get dressed.

ANNIE. No, Frank. I'm the one who has to go.

FRANK. Why?

ANNIE. I...I...can't tell you.

FRANK. Arrrgh!

ANNIE. I can't, Frank. Please. If you go with me, I'll explain maybe. Otherwise, I'm going alone.

FRANK. Like this? You're just going to...run away, without even saying goodbye?

ANNIE. They can't. Say. Goodbye! They'd never understand! They haven't even said goodbye to Robbie yet.

FRANK. Well, I'm part of the problem here. Maybe I can help.

ANNIE. ...How?

FRANK. The situation is complex. What we need here...is a really, really bizarre plan.

ANNIE. ...So?

FRANK. So I'm going to have to sleep on it.

ANNIE. I'll never get out of here.

FRANK. Yes you will. I'll figure something out. Just leave it to me, okay?

ANNIE. Okay. ...Tomorrow.

FRANK. Fine.

ANNIE. Morning.

FRANK. Morning. Deal?

ANNIE. ...Deal.

They shake hands. **ANNIE** *turns to go back to bed, but* **FRANK** *pulls her toward him. She kisses his cheek and trudges off to the bedroom.* **FRANK** *sits down on the couch, exhausted.*

FRANK. ...Alright. Okay. Can do.

He blinks back the sleepiness and starts thinking. End scene.

Scene 4

At rise: later that night. It is still raining outside.
FRANK *is still sitting on the couch – but he's fast asleep,*
his mouth hanging open. **GEORGE** *sneaks in from the*
kitchen, dressed for fishing and carrying beers.

GEORGE. Pssst. Pssssssssssst. Hey, Franky boy! Get up! Let's
go! The fish'll eat without us. Frank!

FRANK. Ooooooh noooooo.

GEORGE. Come on, sun's almost up!

FRANK. Nooo, nooo, noooooo.

GEORGE. That's the spirit. Up we go.

FRANK. Doesn't anyone around here sleep?

GEORGE. Not when there's fishing to do. Come on! We
gotta hurry before mother gets up.

FRANK. George, I'm naked.

GEORGE. I stole your pants.

He produces them and begins to try to dress **FRANK**.

FRANK. I'm hungry.

GEORGE. Have a beer.

FRANK. I'm wounded.

GEORGE. Tough it out. Come on, Franky boy, pick up your
leg!

FRANK. I can't. No way. My fishing days are over.

GEORGE. What are you talkin'? You love fishing. *We* love
fishing.

FRANK. Fish stink. I hate them. No more fishing, ever ever
ever.

GEORGE. Did my wife, did that, has she been talking to
you?

FRANK. I had a vision.

GEORGE. Fool old woman. Can't trust her for a second. I
wake up this morning, got a pillowcase loaded with
fish. I pull on my clothes, got fish heads in my pockets,

fish heads in my sleeves, fish heads in my shoes. She's got big problems. You stick with me.

FRANK. No, I told you. I made up my mind. I don't want to go fishing. All I want to do is –

An idea strikes him.

...George, all I want to do is get out of here. If I had the use of my body, I'd throw it out the door.

GEORGE. Come on! This ain't you talkin'. Buck up!

FRANK. I'm not bucking – .

GEORGE. Let's go bag us a few dykes, sit around a camp-fire, have a good old fashion fish fry. A regular family outing! Be good for us all! What do you say?

FRANK. What do I say? What do I say? Well...let's see. Do I say, "okay, Pop! That's swell!" Or do I say, "Golly, dad, can I have the first shot?" Is that what I say?

GEORGE. ...Well...what are you saying, son?

FRANK. I'm sorry, George, but I'm not your son. ...And you're not my family.

GEORGE. Well, I...I know that, I.... Come on, now. I thought you and me...I thought we –

FRANK. Well we're not, okay? We're not.

GEORGE. ...That's no way to talk, now. ...You come in here, take our kindness and protection –

FRANK. Protection!

GEORGE. That's not the kind of appreciation we deserve. Look at me when I'm talking to you! ...Is this your way of saying thanks to a man who...who only wanted to be your friend? Or a, or a family trying to help you along? We're a damned good family – you hear me? But if you don't give a damn about us, fine, you just throw yourself out that door! We don't need you! Or I swear to God I'll shoot you for trespassing.

GEORGE *grabs his shotgun.*

FRANK. Trespassing?

GEORGE. That's right.

FRANK. I'm a hostage here. The only way out is the way Robbie found!

GEORGE. His name ain't Robbie!

FRANK. Neither is mine!

> GEORGE *swings the shotgun and hits* **FRANK** *hard in the head.* **FRANK** *goes down on the floor – out cold. Pause.* **GEORGE** *stands over him.*

GEORGE. ...Damn you, boy. Damn you!

> *He stands over* **FRANK,** *shaking. End scene.*

Scene 5

In darkness: the rain stops.

At rise: morning. The sun is coming out. We hear a few birds. FRANK *is lying on the floor where he fell, but has been completely covered up with the afghan.* GEORGE *is standing on the porch, holding his shotgun, staring out into the wilderness. When that picture is established,* ZEE *enters happily from the bedroom, dressed for the day.*

ZEE. Good morning, Frank! Rise and shine. – George? … George?

No response from GEORGE. *She turns back to* FRANK.

Frank, dear, have you seen – ? …Oh, look at you, out like a light! What a dear.
– George!

She finds GEORGE *on the porch and joins him.*

Oh. There you are. What are you doing?

GEORGE. …Nothing.

ZEE. Look at that. The rain has stopped. Looks like it's going to be a beautiful day, doesn't it. …George? …Is something wrong?

GEORGE. No.

ZEE. What are you looking at?

GEORGE. Nothing. …Nothing.

ZEE. …It's the fish heads, isn't it.

GEORGE. …No

ZEE. …I'm sorry about that.

GEORGE. It's not the fish heads.

ZEE. Well, you have to admit it was kind of funny…. George, I said I was sorry. Honestly, you're like a little boy sometimes.

GEORGE. Nothin' wrong with bein' a little boy.

ZEE. …Do you want to tell me something, George? … Georgy-weorgy? Georgy-weorgy-peorgy-deorgy?

She jabs at him playfully.

GEORGE. Don't – don't touch me.

ZEE. ...Has something happened? ...You can tell me.

GEORGE. No I can't.

ZEE. Yes you can. Come inside and tell me.

GEORGE. Don't touch me, dammit! You're always touching! Everything has to be touched! Not me! Just leave me be!

ZEE. George! You tell me what you did this instant!

Pause. **GEORGE** *grapples with it.*

GEORGE. ...I didn't want him to go away, Zee. ...I didn't want him to go.

ZEE *understands something. She enters the cabin slowly, cautiously, smiling even. She approaches* **FRANK** *but never actually touches him; instead she circles his body, reaching, withdrawing.*

ZEE. ...Frank? ...Frank dear. Frank? ...Oh my God. Frank? Baby?

GEORGE *is still on the porch, staring out.*

GEORGE. It's not my fault! It's your fault! You did it to him! He was your boy! Nobody else could touch him!

ZEE. Frank dear? Frank! Wake up, baby!

GEORGE. Don't touch him! It's too late! Just leave him be!

ZEE. Oh God! Do something, George!

GEORGE. He's dead! ...It's too late. He's dead.... He's....

ZEE *weakens, sits on the couch over the body. She is too stunned to cry.* **GEORGE** *stands silently on the porch. Pause. Finally,* **ANNIE** *enters in her robe.*

ANNIE. Why is everyone yelling?

ZEE. Yelling? No one's yelling. Everything's...everything's fine.

ANNIE. Is something wrong, Mama?

ZEE. Wrong? No, no! Nothing's…. Well, Frank's dead. Your father killed him. That's not good.

ANNIE looks at FRANK's body. She is incredulous.

ANNIE. What? …Oh, come on!

ZEE. Oh yes.

ANNIE. For God's sake – Frank, of all the idiot – !

She kicks the body.

ZEE. Annie!

ANNIE. Get up! Knock it off! This isn't funny!

She kicks him again. **ZEE** *tries to pull her away.*

ZEE. Annie! Stop that!

ANNIE. It's alright, Mother, he's – oh God!

ANNIE has pulled back the blanket. **FRANK**'s *head is bloodied and his eyes are closed.*

…Oh my God! Frank? Frank!

She reaches for him; **ZEE** *pulls her back.*

ZEE. Annie, no, baby. No.

ANNIE. Frank! No! Get up! Frank! Please!

ZEE. Shhh! Shhh, Annie!

ANNIE wheels away from **ZEE** *and runs off to the kitchen. Pause.* **GEORGE** *comes in from the porch and skulks into the room.*

GEORGE. …Well?

ZEE. …Well what?

GEORGE. I don't know what to say.

ZEE. Huh!

GEORGE. …It was an accident.

ZEE. An accident. *Whoops.*

GEORGE. It was, Zee.

ZEE. I'm not saying anything.

GEORGE. Please, Zee. Please.

ANNIE *enters with a wet cloth, crosses to* **FRANK**, *cradles his head and begins to clean the blood from his face.*

Zee? ...Please.

ZEE. What do you want from me? Do you want me to say it's alright? We've killed another one, George!

GEORGE. I know! I'm sorry!

ZEE. You're sorry! What good is that, you're sorry? What do we do with sorry? Just pretend it never happened? That's okay. Daddy's sorry. No hard feelings. All better now!

ANNIE. Mama, don't.

ZEE. (*angrily, to* **ANNIE**) Do you want to know what he did that night after...brutalizing my son? After taking him out to the garage and making him swill beer? After beating him till he –

GEORGE. I never hurt my boy! I never hurt him!

ZEE. You –

GEORGE. *He was my son! He was my son!*

Pause. **GEORGE** *is almost curled up in pain.*

...I was only trying to...to *help* him, Zee! It was the only way I knew. I would never...I'd never hurt my boy.

ZEE. He was a child.

GEORGE. He was trying to become a man! ...And you wouldn't let him. He needed me!

ANNIE. Daddy.

ZEE. ...He came in to our room...to our bed....

GEORGE. ...the only way I knew.

ZEE. And he lay there. I could hear him.

GEORGE. Please, Zee. He needed me.

ZEE. Weeping. Like a child.

(**GEORGE** *collapses to his knees, perhaps leaning on the shotgun*)

And I was supposed to just lay there, pretending not to hear.... While out there. My son. My baby. Was leaving me. Why? …Why did he…? He never even… said goodbye.

GEORGE. Please Zee! Forgive me…. Forgive me…..

He weeps. ZEE *cradles his head.*

ZEE. Shhhhh.

GEORGE. He was my son too….

ZEE. I know. Shhhh.

ZEE *hums, sadly. Pause:* ZEE *holds* GEORGE, ANNIE *cradles* FRANK*'s body. Then:*

ANNIE. …Daddy? It's not your fault. … Mama?

ZEE *continues humming, rocking* GEORGE *gently.*

…He came to my room that night, to my room… Mama? Listen to me!

ZEE *does.*

…I could have stopped him. But I didn't. He told me he was leaving, and I said…I said good. Go! Just go! He wanted me to come with him, but I said get out! Just… leave us all alone!

ANNIE *releases* FRANK *and backs away.* ZEE *will move toward her, and* GEORGE *will stand and lean his gun against the couch.*

And he looked at me so…sorry and so confused that…I don't think I'm ever going to forget. …I could have stopped him, Mama. But I was…I was sick of him! I was sick of one more night spent fighting over poor, weak, stupid, little Robbie!

This is too much: ZEE *steps closer and raises her hand to slap* ANNIE, *but stops when:*

GEORGE. (*without moving*) Zee.

ANNIE *stands, awaiting the punishment.*

ANNIE. It's my fault, Mama.

ZEE *reaches out, touches* ANNIE*'s cheek, and draws*

ANNIE *toward her. They embrace.*

…It's all my fault. I didn't mean it –

ZEE. No, no, no.

ANNIE. – I didn't want him to –

ZEE. Annie, how could you have known? How could…any of us?

GEORGE. Why didn't you say something.

ANNIE. I didn't…I….

ZEE. It's alright now. Shhh. It's alright. You're our angel.

ANNIE. No, no –

ZEE. You are. You've always been our angel. Isn't that right, George?

GEORGE. …That's right, Bucky.

ZEE. It…it was an accident. It was an accident, isn't that right, George?

GEORGE. …It was. …It was.

He turns to **FRANK***'s body. They all do. Pause.*

ZEE. …Well? What do we do now?

GEORGE. I don't know…. But I bet we don't get any trick-or-treaters for years.

ZEE. How do we say it happened?

GEORGE. We'll just…we'll just… say it happened. … Sometimes –

ZEE. Sometimes these things…sometimes the best intentions….

GEORGE. That's right.

ZEE. Isn't that right, Annie?

ANNIE. …Mmm-hmm.

Pause.

ZEE. …We'll all rot in jail and never see each other again. Won't we George?

GEORGE. Yup.

ZEE *is overcome. She turns and exits to the porch.*

GEORGE kisses ANNIE's forehead and joins ZEE on the porch. We see them there, comforting one another. Alone with FRANK's body, ANNIE speaks softly, sadly.

ANNIE. ...Well, you did it, didn't you. It's over. It's all over.

She kneels and kisses FRANK's head and covers him up. Then she rises and exits to the kitchen. Pause.

Finally, FRANK stirs a little beneath the blanket and groans.

FRANK. ...Oooooooh. ...Ooooooooooooohhh.

GEORGE and ZEE, hearing it, look at each other and race inside. FRANK sits up, still beneath the blanket.

...Ooooooooooohhhhh.

GEORGE. Zee!

ZEE. Frank? Frank! Oh my – !

They uncover him. FRANK sees them:

FRANK. Ooooooh God!

ZEE. Annie! Annie!

GEORGE. He's alive! He's alive!

ZEE. Don't try to get up.

GEORGE. Let him stand!

ANNIE enters. FRANK is crawling away from them.

ZEE. He's too weak!

GEORGE. It's better if he tries!

ZEE. Why, so you can knock him down again?

GEORGE. Don't start with me! He's got to get the blood flowing!

ZEE. It is! Right out of his head! Annie – get some water. Somebody – start a fire!

FRANK. Get back! Stay back!

GEORGE. He's trying to get up! Let him go!

ZEE. You let him go!

Another tug-of-war begins. FRANK shakes himself free.

FRANK. Don't touch me! Either of you!

ZEE. Your head is bleeding!

FRANK. Let it bleed! I want it to bleed! I like it!

ZEE. He's dazed.

FRANK. (*dazed*) I'm not dazed.

ZEE. Sit down and let us help you.

GEORGE. Try walking around.

> **FRANK** *grabs the shotgun.*

FRANK. Just stay back! Both of you! Nobody touch me or I'll shoot!

ZEE. But you're hurt!

FRANK. No shit (*or "kidding"*), lady, he hit me with this!

GEORGE. I can explain that.

FRANK. I ain't interested!

ZEE. Would you like some breakfast?

FRANK. I'd rather starve!

GEORGE. Please, son, we feel bad enough.

FRANK. So do I! I'm a wreck! I'm getting out of here while I still can!

ZEE. But...you can't go! I haven't fixed your pants!

FRANK. I'll tough it out!

GEORGE. It's flooded out there!

FRANK. *Duh!*

ZEE. You'll drown and get malaria! It's no place for a boy!

FRANK. I'm not a boy, lady. And I'm tired of acting like one. You are very, very strange people and I'm leaving right now! ...Oh yeah: and I'm taking Annie too.

ANNIE. Umm.

FRANK. As a *hostage*! Nobody try anything!

ZEE. You can't!

ANNIE. Um, Frank?

FRANK. Let me handle this.

ANNIE. Maybe this isn't –

FRANK. I'm improvising here, okay?

ZEE. You can't take her!

FRANK. Stay back! I'm desperate!

ZEE. George, *do* something!

GEORGE. He's got the gun!

ANNIE. Frank, I'm in my jammies, I haven't combed my hair or brushed my –

FRANK. Just grab your stuff and let's blow. – Say goodbye everybody!

ANNIE goes to the hope chest and gets her pack.

ZEE. (*desperately*) ...Annie?

ANNIE faces her parents. They look pathetic. Pause.

FRANK. ...Come on, Annie. Surf's up.

ANNIE. Mama? ...Daddy?

FRANK. This is it, Annie. To hell with it, remember? – You two, quit looking at her!

He takes ANNIE's arm.

ANNIE. Let me go.

FRANK. What do you mean, let you go. Let's get out of here before they turn into bats.

ANNIE. They need me, Frank. ...I need them.

FRANK. Don't say it!

ANNIE. ...I can't go.

FRANK. I knew it! I knew it! This is just *great!*

ANNIE. I'm sorry, Frank.

GEORGE. We're all sorry. You've got to forgive us.

ZEE. That's all we want.

GEORGE. Please? Frank? ...Son?

Pause. FRANK looks at them.

FRANK. ...Oh, no. No no no no no no you don't. I see what's going on here. Ten years from now, right here, scars all over my body. Nuh-uh-uh-uh, just give me my coat before something else happens.

GEORGE *retrieves his coat and gives it to him.*

ZEE. Help him with it.

FRANK. I can do it! ...What else? My pack. Give me my pack.

ZEE gets his pack from wherever she's hidden it.

ZEE. It's heavy.

FRANK. I'll manage.

GEORGE. Do you need any money?

ZEE. Or a snack? I could make you a nice fish sandwich.

FRANK. Just cut it out! You *maniacs*!

ZEE. We can't let you go like this!

GEORGE. Isn't there something we can do?

ZEE. Let us help you.

FRANK. I don't need any help. You do. Help yourselves! Now I'm gonna hike up to the bait shop, catch a ride, and go home! So my *own* parents can kill me. Got it?

GEORGE *and* **ZEE** *nod, conceding.*

...Okay.

FRANK *exits through the front door, wearing his coat, carrying his pack and the gun, and slams the door. He takes three steps onto the porch, realizes he's in his stocking feet, swears under his breath, and re-enters.*

...Shoes.

ZEE scurries to the couch, where she's hidden them under a cushion.

ZEE. Oh. Over here. I was drying them.

FRANK. Great.

GEORGE. Do you need any rubbers?

They all look at **GEORGE,** *bewildered.*

...Boots! Rubber boots!

FRANK. Aw, God.

GEORGE holds the galoshes while FRANK slides his stocking feet into them. ZEE gets the afghan and holds it up – it's full of holes, including one big one in the middle.

ZEE. And here. You need this.

FRANK. Why?

ZEE. Security.

She pulls the afghan over FRANK's head like a poncho. Now he is standing there, holding his shoes, his pack, the shotgun, wearing rubber boots and a poncho, looking ridiculous.

FRANK. ...Is that it? We got everything? ...Okay. Now I'm going out the door here. And nothing can stop me. Don't expect any Christmas cards or anything. Okay? ...Sheesh!

He turns to go, but:

ZEE. ...Frank?

He turns, sees ZEE standing there meek and hopeful, sighs, and holds his arms open so she can run up and hug him.

...God bless you child. God bless you.

They part. FRANK looks at GEORGE, standing there sheepishly. He sighs and holds out the shotgun. GEORGE takes it and nods, understanding the gesture, but looks at it dubiously. FRANK turns to go.

GEORGE. ...Frank? ...There's...there's wild dogs in these hills.

He hold the shotgun back out to FRANK. FRANK understands, smiles and takes it back. Then he surveys the group.

FRANK. ...Okay. ...So I guess that's it, right?

No answer.

...Rrrrright.

He turns and exits slowly, closing the front door behind him. At the last second, **ANNIE** *calls:*

ANNIE. Frank?

> **FRANK** *bolts back in the door. They run together and hug tightly.*

...Be careful.

FRANK. Yeah, you *too.*

> *He's about to kiss her – but sees* **GEORGE** *and* **ZEE** *standing there, watching. So he lets her go, and faces them all one last time.*

...Well. ...Okay. ...Goodbye?

> *He smiles.* **ZEE** *nods and waves meekly. Fondly now:*

...Goodbye.

> *He exits through the door, off the porch, and is gone. Long pause.*

GEORGE. ...Well! Interesting fella!

> **ZEE** *runs to the window.*

ZEE. What if a tree falls on him? Or a boulder or something? What if he gets lost or falls off a cliff or –

ANNIE. Mama.

> *Pause.* **ZEE** *shrugs, cheers up.*

ZEE. Oh. ...Well. What do we now?

GEORGE. The roads are bad. Mud's too deep for the Camry. Have to wait till it dries up.

ZEE. How long will that take.

GEORGE. Don't know. Doesn't matter though. We got plenty to do. Maybe go catch us a few snakes, eh Bucky?

ZEE. Snakes?

ANNIE. *Daddy.*

GEORGE. What say we start havin' some fun, like we came up here for.

ZEE. ...We could roast marshmallows.

GEORGE. That's right. Over an open fire.

ZEE. That's right! ...Except that wood won't burn.

GEORGE. Oh yeah.

ZEE. And we're out of marshmallows.

Gloom. They sit on the couch, **ANNIE** *in the middle.*

GEORGE. ...That's okay. We...we got everything we need. Isn't that right?

ZEE. That's right. We do. And we needed a good rain, isn't that right, Annie?

ANNIE. Yes we did, Mama.

Pause. Sigh. **GEORGE** *pats his legs decisively and stands.*

GEORGE. ...Well!

ZEE. Where are you going?

GEORGE. ...Out to bury Fritz.

ZEE. ...Oh yeah. And we'll have to call the Keefers, you know.

GEORGE. I knooow.

He leaves and exits the porch. **ZEE** *stands and follows him.*

ZEE. (*as she leaves*) And don't touch it, George. It has diseases. Get a stick or a plastic bag or something.

GEORGE. (*off*) I knooooowww.

ZEE. (*off*) Is there a shovel? I didn't see a shovel. Are you sure that it's dead?

GEORGE. (*off*) Yeeeesss I'm suuuure.

ZEE. (*off*) How do you know? What are you going to do with it? We can't bury it, it's not our property, George....

And so on, while **ANNIE** *sits on the couch, cringing and smiling. Fade to black. End of play.*

PROPERTIES

Two afghans - one with a hole "blasted" in the center, one without
One or more balls of yarn
One set of knitting needles
One bloody carcass of a small dog, wearing a collar
One or more throw pillows
One vase or other breakable decoration
One shotgun with one blank shell
Two icepacks
One backpack
One can of Spaghettio's
One box full of fishing flies
One book: Walden, by Henry David Thoreau
One fishing license
One man's flannel shirt
One bottle of alcohol
Assorted bandages: ace or gauze wrap
Assorted dishes: coffee cup, plate for fish, etc.
Eight or ten full beer cans
One empty beer can
One fishing stringer, loaded with 10-20 empty beer cans
One fishing "fly"
Five to ten small logs
Two or three towels
A needle—or a sewing basket with a needle
A pair of galoshes/rubber boots
Fish and "bloody" pieces of fish (rubber or otherwise)
One small living room rug
One travel bag or pack
A man's coat
Matches
One minnow (rubber or otherwise)
One "Star Trek Travel Mug," with lid
One first aid kit, with bandages
One plate of scrambled eggs
One pillow and pillow case
One wet washcloth